This Little Tiger book belongs to:

_____

_____

_____

"Tiger, will you look after Cub?

He'll be as good as gold. Bye!"

Jonny Lambert

Tiger Tiger

"Bother!"

LITTLE TIGER PRESS
London

Cub stared at Tiger.
Tiger frowned at Cub.
Slump! Flump!
"Bother!" growled Tiger.
"I'm too old for cub-sitting."

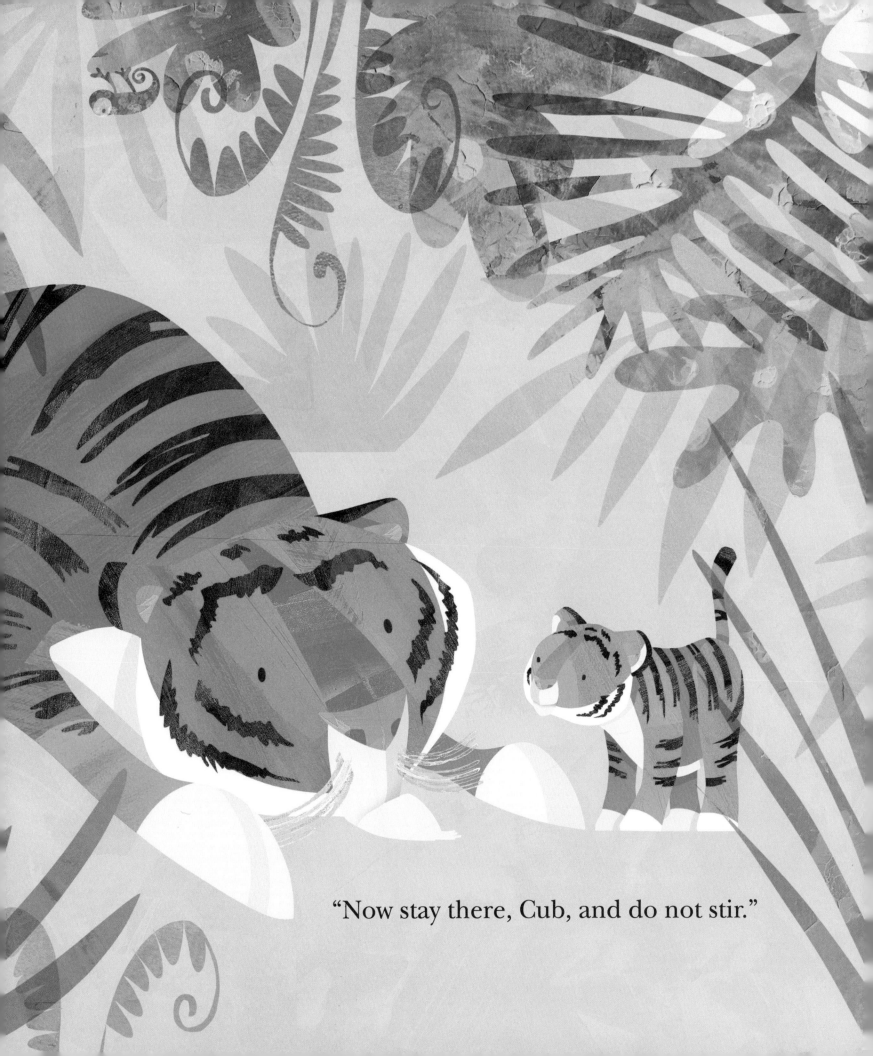

"Now stay there, Cub, and do not stir."

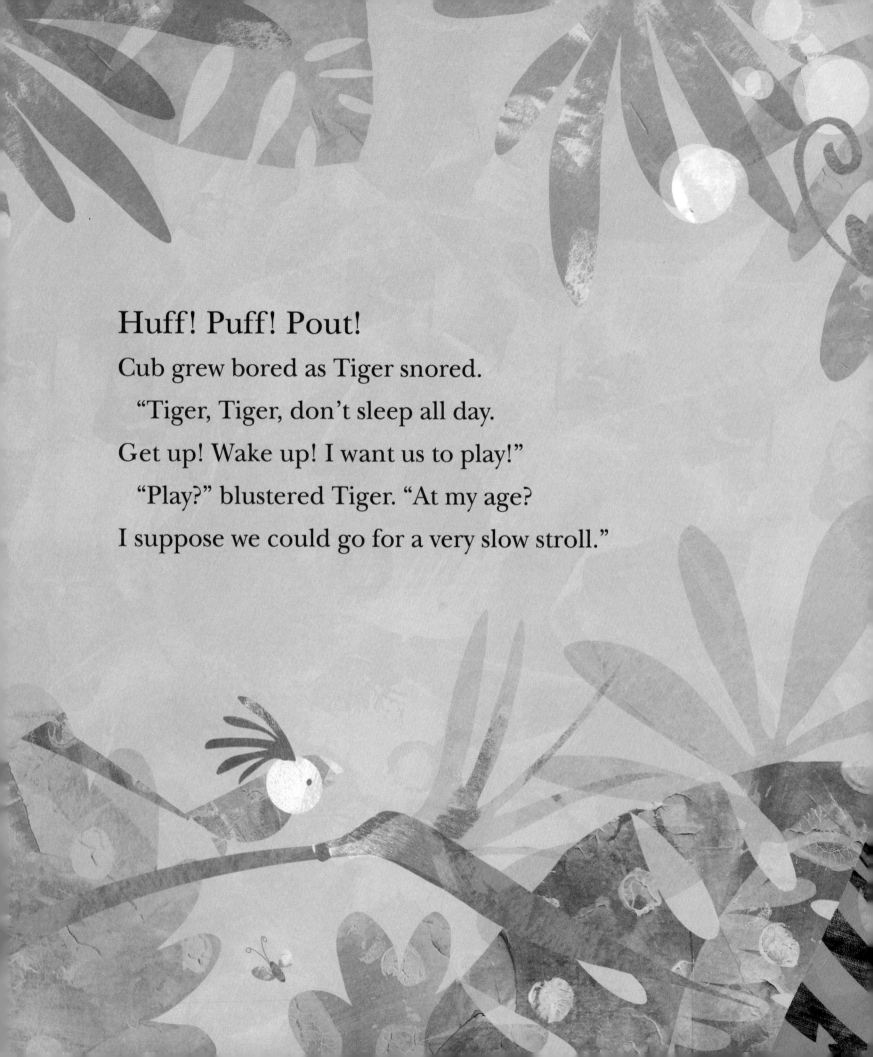

Huff! Puff! Pout!

Cub grew bored as Tiger snored.

"Tiger, Tiger, don't sleep all day.

Get up! Wake up! I want us to play!"

"Play?" blustered Tiger. "At my age?

I suppose we could go for a very slow stroll."

Dart! Dash! Rush!

Cub ran along the jungle trail.

Tiger followed, nose to tail.

"Tiger, Tiger, come on! Let's run!

I want to explore. I want to have FUN!"

"Piffle," muttered Tiger. "It's too
hot to explore. And there's nothing
to see around here any more."

Flit! Float! Flutter!

The butterfly gleamed and Cub beamed.

"Tiger, Tiger, look what I've found.

Down here! SEE? On the ground!"

"Humbrum," tutted Tiger. "That's just a grub.
Right, it's time to go back and nap now, Cub."

Chit-chat! Yatter!

Monkeys swung to and fro.

"But Tiger, Tiger, there's so much to see.

Look up! Yes, up! High in the tree!"

"Puffle! I see them," mumbled Tiger.
"I remember that noisy lot!"

Bristle! Sniff! Twitch!

"Cub, Cub, don't make a sound!"

Tiger snarled and stood his ground.

Crawl! Creep! Crouch!
"Stay close to me," Tiger whispered,
moving quietly.

Snort! Stomp! Crashing through,
two tiny rhinos romped into view.
    "Gosh!" Tiger exclaimed. "Baby rhinos!
How rare! Cub, Cub, there was nothing
to fear . . ."

Tiger turned, but Cub wasn't there!

Clasp! Claw! Clamber!
Cub climbed excitedly
high up the nearest tree.
  "Tiger, Tiger, look!
Above me . . . Who is this?
She looks so funny!"

"Oh my!" smiled Tiger. "You've found Pangolin. But Cub, Cub, come back down. Here, where it's safe. On the ground!"

Cling! Grasp! Grip!

Cub held on tight, squeaking with delight.

"NO! I WON'T! You can't catch me.

I'm a fast climber. Look! See!"

Spring! Jump! Catch!

"Aha!" laughed Tiger. "Not quite quick enough!
Cub, that was FUN. Now, would you like to
see Sambar deer . . ."

"…RUN!"

Startled by the stripy old cat, the grazing deer
scattered this way and that.

Leap! Laugh! Giggle!
Bouncing along the jungle trail,
Tiger chased Cub, nose to tail.

"Tiger, Tiger, can we explore some more?"
Cub didn't want the day to end.
Tiger smiled. "Of course we can . . ."

"…my little friend."

To Samuel – the adventure begins
~ J L

LITTLE TIGER PRESS
1 The Coda Centre,
189 Munster Road, London SW6 6AW
www.littletiger.co.uk

First published in Great Britain 2017
This edition published 2017

Text and illustrations copyright © Jonny Lambert 2017
Jonny Lambert has asserted his right to be
identified as the author and illustrator of this work
under the Copyright, Designs and Patents Act, 1988

Printed in China • LTP/1800/1658/0816

2 4 6 8 10 9 7 5 3 1

More stunning books from
Jonny Lambert!

THE GREAT
AAA
-OOO!

I love you
more
and more

Little
Why

For information regarding any of the above titles
or for our catalogue, please contact us:
Little Tiger Press, 1 The Coda Centre,
189 Munster Road, London SW6 6AW
Tel: 020 7385 6333
E-mail: contact@littletiger.co.uk
www.littletiger.co.uk